THE SNARK!

For all the parents.
The unsung heroes that scare
away the monsters!

Find me on
every page!

Published in the United Kingdom by:

Blue Falcon Publishing
The Mill, Pury Hill Business Park,
Alderton Road, Towcester
Northamptonshire NN12 7LS
Email: books@bluefalconpublishing.co.uk
Web: www.bluefalconpublishing.co.uk

A CIP record of this book is available from the British Library.

First printed November 2020
Available in hardback, paperback and as an ebook.

ISBN 9781912765058

Other books by
Justin Davis

My Bunny

Follow Millie, a young girl who just loves her bunny – so much so that he must go everywhere with her. The trouble is, he keeps going missing! Join in the hunt as Millie searches for her favourite long-eared, round-tummied companion!

*'A captivating, sweetly illustrated story. A **finalist** and highly recommended.'* **The Wishing Shelf Book Awards**

A Pirate's Song

A lively rhyming picture book will have children singing along with the pirates on their journey. Will they find their gold?

Ahoy there, me hearties! Are ye brave? Are ye strong? Can ye sing **A Pirate's Song**? Will ye search for treasures old, jewels and trinkets, pearls and gold? Then climb aboard and join our crew! Quickly now, there's work to do!

The Fearless Four *(an illustrated chapter series)*

Escape from Nettle Farm, Book 1

When Harvey the Newfoundland puppy is rescued from an unpleasant fate by the Baker family, he couldn't be more content. He finally has the loving home he dreamed of.

But if he thinks he's in for a quiet life, he had better think again! Join Harvey and the Baker family in this thrilling adventure series.

Spy Danger, Book 2

The Baker children can't believe their luck when they find out they are staying at a castle for the weekend. But when they uncover a plot to steal forgotten treasures, Millie, Jamie, Zach and their dog Harvey know they have to act. Are they smart enough to outwit the thieves? Can they decode the clues in time? Or has their spying put them in too much danger?

About the Author

The Snark is the fifth publication from Northamptonshire-based Justin Davis. His previous books have attracted praise and won him a rapidly growing young fanbase. Escape from Nettle Farm, the prequel to Spy Danger, won a **Red Ribbon** in **The Wishing Shelf Book Awards 2016** and was a **finalist** in the **People's Book Prize 2017**. **My Bunny**, a beautifully illustrated rhyming picture book, was a **finalist** in **The Wishing Shelf Book Awards 2017**.

Follow me | Facebook/Instagram @authorjustindavis | Twitter @jdavisauthor
www.justindavis.co.uk

This book belongs to

_____

Justin Davis

Quite some time ago, before you were born, someone told a story. It became a favourite bedtime tale, shared while the little ones were tucked up safe and sound in bed.

Although the story was a **tiny bit scary**, it was funny, too! The little ones would **gasp** and **laugh** and **snuggle** down under their duvets and say, **"Please tell us more!"**

They weren't really scared because they knew it was only a story. There was no such thing, really... no such thing...

as the Snark!

"What's a Snark?" I hear you cry.
A fearless beast who lurks nearby!

He's big - no, **huge!**
As huge as a house,
yet moves as **quick** as
a **little** white mouse.

I hear him coming, the Snark is near -
it's time that I was **out of here!**

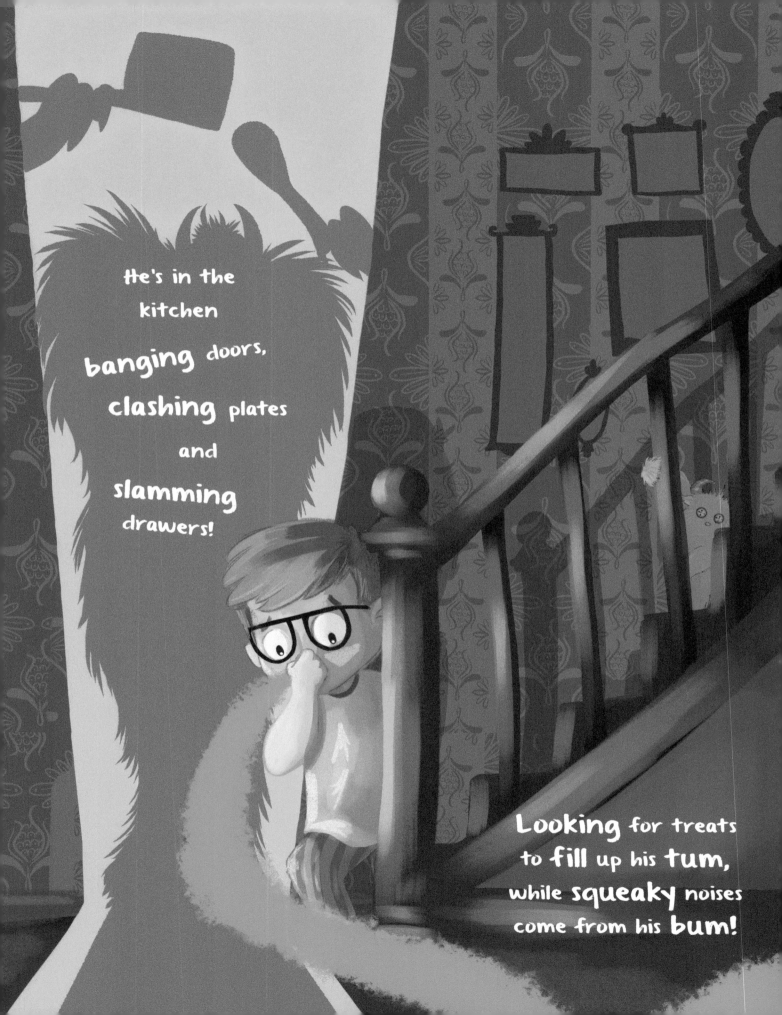

He's in the kitchen
banging doors,
clashing plates
and
slamming
drawers!

Looking for treats
to fill up his tum,
while squeaky noises
come from his bum!

Pump! Zing! Parp! Guff!

He fills the room with stinky stuff!

No wonder I'm so scared of the dark. That's when it's feeding time for the Snark!

"What's a Snark?" I hear you cry.
A **fearless** beast who's **slinking** by!

He's big - no, **huge!** As huge as a house,
yet moves as quick as a little white mouse.
He has two **little ears** and a big **fat nose**,
with two **beady eyes** to see where he goes.
I hear him coming, the Snark is near -
it's time that I was **out of here!**

A **creaking** sound comes from the **stairs.**

I **think** it's time to say my **prayers.**

When I **hear** his steps like **thunder**,
I grab my duvet and **climb under!**
What's that **smell?** It's really grotty.
It must be coming from **Snark's botty!**

The **Snark** is ready for his tea,

and I'm **afraid** it might be... **me!**

"What's a Snark?"
I hear you cry.
A **fearless** beast
who's **creeping by!**

He's big - no, **huge!** As huge as a house,
yet moves as **quick** as a little white mouse.
He has two **little ears** and a big **fat nose,**
with two **beady eyes** to see where he goes.

He turns the handle
to my room.
I dare to squint
into the gloom.

I hold onto my **teddy** tight in case the **beast** gives him a **fright!**

"What's a Snark?" I hear you cry.
A fearless beast who's sneaking by!
He's big - no, huge! As huge as a house,
yet moves as quick as a little white mouse.
He has two little ears and a big fat nose,
with two beady eyes to see where he goes.
His wiry beard is long and hairy;
I hear his roar - it's really scary!

Two
long legs
and
two
flat feet;
I wonder who
he wants
to eat?

I hear
him
coming,
the
Snark
is near -
it's
time
that I
was
out
of
here!

I feel him **leaning**
very **near**
and hear him **breathing**
in my **ear**.

I see his shadow
looming close,
his botty smells
are really gross!

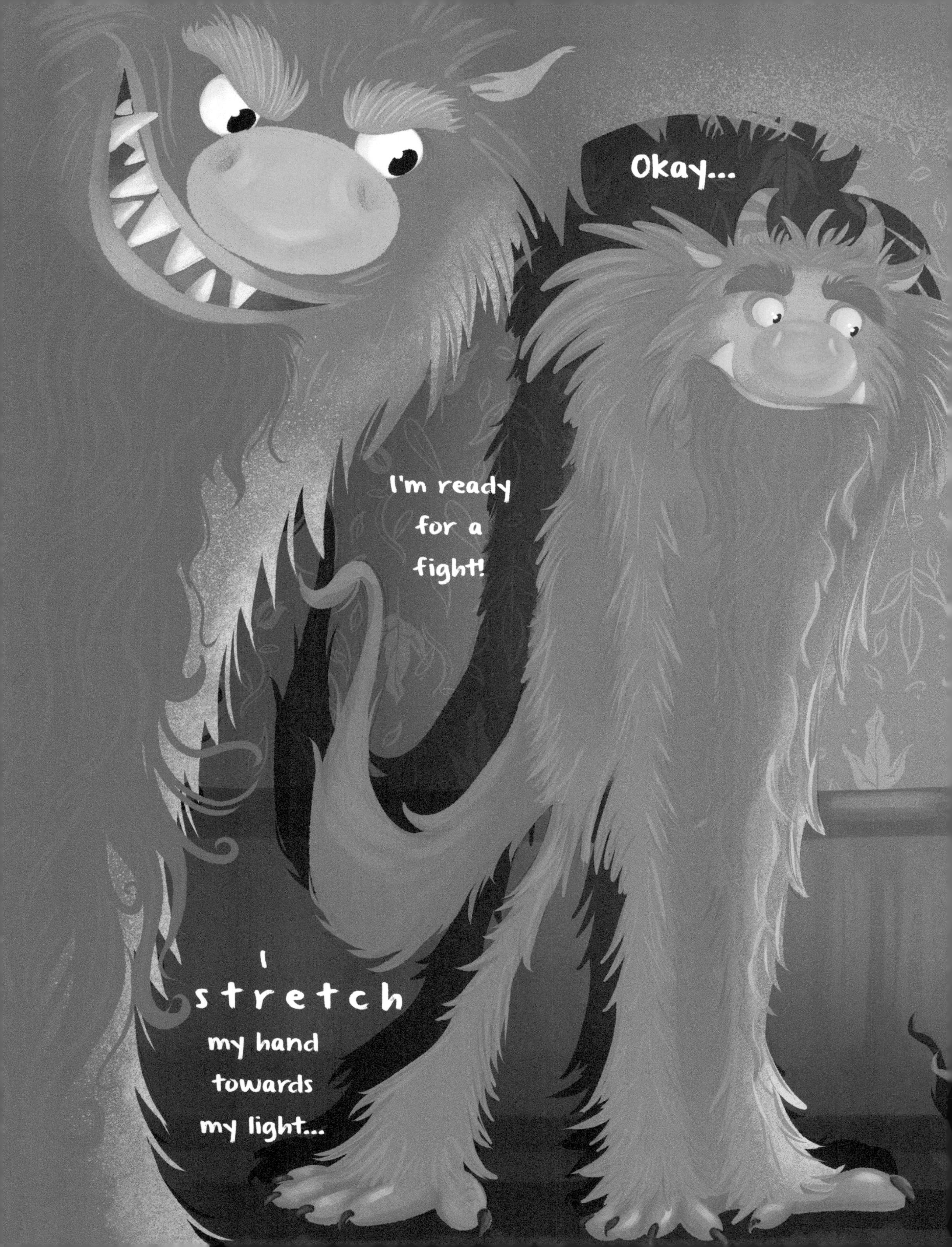
Okay...
I'm ready for a fight!
I stretch my hand towards my light...

I flick the switch,
and then...
oh, phew!

"Hi Dad,
I'm really glad
it's you!"

Let's make a monster!

Look how monsters can be drawn using simple shapes.

FLUFFY?

SPIKY?

CURLY?

NOSES

TEETH

Draw your own monster!

Use this page or get a blank sheet of paper and draw your own monster.

Lightning Source UK Ltd.
Milton Keynes UK
UKHW021157201120
373751UK00007B/148